TONY BRADMAN

013958163 6

First published in 2012 in Great Britain by
Barrington Stoke Ltd
18 Walker Street, Edinburgh, EH3 7LP

www.barringtonstoke.co.uk

Reprinted 2013

ISBN: 978-1-78112-073-6

Printed in China by Leo

Contents

Chapter 1
The Lady of the Lake

Merlin came round the last bend in the narrow track and saw a small lake with rocks all round the edge. He knew this was the right place. There was a tall snow-capped mountain beyond the lake and Merlin could see it reflected in the lake's smooth water. The sun was setting, and in the east the sky was beginning to grow dark.

It had taken Merlin months to find this spot. Had he really found the place he wanted? He'd walked all over Britain, and had come at last to this lake in the far north. He was in the land of the wild Picts and the hills were cold and bare.

Merlin hadn't been a wizard very long and over the last year his life had been full of surprises. He had a feeling there were lots more to come ...

"Well, there's no point in hanging about," he said to himself. "The sooner I get down there and ask my question, the sooner I can go home."

Until a year ago, Merlin had been just a poor boy living in a village with his mother. Then one day a messenger had ridden into the village and told him that King Vortigern, The High King of Britain, wanted to see him. Vortigern was a fool, and not much of a king. But because of him, Merlin had found out what his true destiny was.

A red dragon lived under the King's castle, and the dragon had helped Merlin unleash the magic within him. The dragon had told Merlin it was his job to save Britain from the Saxons. Every day more and more Saxons raided Britain from the sea. They were fierce and cruel. They burnt the villages and took the land for themselves. The Britons were driven further and further inland.

Merlin's magic was strong, but not strong enough to fight the Saxons.

That's why he was here now, standing beside this strange lake. He wanted to be stronger before it was too late. More and more Saxons landed in Britain every day. Like rats, they swarmed over the land. Merlin's last hope was that the Lady of the Lake could help him. He'd read about her in a very old book of magic. In the book, Merlin had read all about the lake, he knew what it looked like, but the book hadn't said where it was. Merlin had found the lake at last. But was the long hunt going to be worth it ...?

"Hear me, Lady of the Lake," he shouted. "I have a question for you."

There was no answer, just the sound of his voice ringing out round the rocks like an owl hooting, "You ... you ... you ..." The sun had dipped down below the hills and a pale moon had risen. Its light cast a silver sheen on the water.

Merlin held his breath and counted to ten. He opened his mouth to call out again, but suddenly something moved in front of him. Some splashes broke the surface of the lake and water lapped at his feet.

A beautiful woman rose slowly from the lake and walked towards him. She stopped at the edge of the water. She had long blonde hair and wore a glowing gown of fine green silk. Silvery drops ran off her, but she didn't look at all wet.

"I hear you, Merlin," she said with a smile. Her voice was soft and low. He saw now that her eyes were the same colour as her dress. "Ask me your question."

"How do you know my name?" Merlin frowned. "You've never met me before."

"Is that your question?" she said. "Be careful, Merlin. I can only answer one question. Is that what you want to know? I think you have something more important on your mind."

"You're right," said Merlin. He felt cross with himself. He should have known he'd need to be careful what he said when he was talking to someone from the worlds of magic.

"Well, what is it, then?" said the lady. "Speak, or leave me to my dreams under the water ..." She began to back away from him and her voice began to get softer and softer.

"No, wait, please!" said Merlin. He stepped further into the lake, the water cold on his legs. "My question is simple – how can I make my magic stronger?"

The lady stopped, and her eyes sparkled in the moonlight. "The answer is simple," she said. "To make yourself stronger ... you must use a ring of power."

In his mind, Merlin saw a picture of a gold ring on a woman's finger. But did the Lady of the Lake mean this sort of ring? Merlin had a feeling her ring was a magic one.

"What do you mean 'a ring of power'?" said Merlin. "Where would I get such a thing? Do you have one I could borrow, or maybe buy?"

"So many questions!" said the lady, and laughed at him. Her voice sounded like an icy river tumbling over rocks. "And I have no more answers for you."

Suddenly she started to back away from him again. The water rose swiftly to her waist. Merlin walked into the water after her. "Tell me more, I beg you!" he called out.

The lady stopped for a moment. The water was up to her chin. "Blue stones," she said softly, or at least that's what Merlin thought she said. "You will need blue stones, Merlin ..."

Then she was gone. The silvery water closed over her head as if she'd never been there. A wisp of mist drifted over the spot where she'd vanished, and the water was still again, as if it was a giant mirror to reflect the stars in the sky. Then a cloud passed in front of the moon, and the lake was dark.

Merlin turned and walked back to the narrow track. He stood there thinking for a moment. He wished that the lady's answer had been more helpful. But then he gave a shrug and stood up tall. There was no point in being gloomy. He had some idea now of what he had to find, and he told himself that he'd find it no matter how difficult that was. But what were blue stones? And how would they help him ...?

Soon Merlin was walking back down the track, away from the lake. He had been away for a long time, and he was keen to return to the castle of the King. He'd have to make sure everything was all right there before he set off to hunt for this ring of power. He only hoped that Vortigern had been behaving himself.

But the King had done something terrible, as Merlin was about to find out ...

Chapter 2
Down in the Dumps

It was a lovely, late spring day when at last Merlin came to the King's castle. The sun was shining as he walked through the main gate – but he knew almost at once that something was wrong. The soldiers on guard didn't look at him, and one of them ran off to see Vortigern as soon as he saw Merlin.

Merlin followed. He took his time and his heart sank. The King was waiting for him in his great hall. Merlin could see he was worried even if Vortigern was trying hard to keep a big grin on his face. Merlin came closer. The hall was crowded with people – servants, warriors, the pagan priests called druids who dressed in black cloaks and looked like giant crows.

"It's wonderful to have you back, Merlin!" said Vortigern. His voice squeaked with nerves. "Er ... did you have a good trip? I can't wait to hear all about it."

"No problem, I'd be happy to tell you," said Merlin. "But first, why don't you tell me what's been going on here? You all seem a bit down in the dumps."

"Down in the dumps? Us?" said Vortigern. "Where did you get that idea from? We're feeling pretty cheerful now the weather's warming up, aren't we, lads?"

The chief druid was standing next to Vortigern. He looked very gloomy. The King gave him a crafty kick. Merlin could see that it hurt but the old man smiled and pretended to be happy. The others did the same.

Merlin gave a sigh and shook his head. "You've never been a good liar, Vortigern," he said. "I can tell you've been up to something stupid – so you'd better let me know the truth before I lose my temper."

Everyone ducked as Merlin lifted his hands and blue sparks crackled from them. Vortigern looked even more nervous now. They'd all seen before what Merlin could do and they knew how the flashes of energy Merlin threw at them hurt.

"All right, I attacked the Saxons!" said the King in a panicky voice. "I know you told me not to, but it was too good a chance to miss. I almost won ..."

"What do you mean, you almost won?" said Merlin. "What happened?"

"A spy told us that King Hengist, the chief of the Saxons, had come into our lands in secret to have a look round. He had some of his men with him," muttered Vortigern. "They camped on the great plain near the great river."

Catching Hengist would have been a real victory for Vortigern. But Hengist was a great warrior, and far too cunning for Vortigern. Vortigern could never have defeated him, even if the Saxon chief only had a few men with him. Vortigern had plenty of brave warriors on his side – but he was totally useless at war.

"I think I can guess what happened," said Merlin. "You rode off without a plan, attacked Hengist, and got badly beaten. How many men did you lose?"

"Not that many," Vortigern said. He began to look shifty again. "Two or three hundred, that's all," he muttered.

"Two or three hundred!'" Merlin said and his eyes burned with anger. "What were you thinking, Vortigern? We can't afford to lose that many men ..."

"What's the problem?" said Vortigern with a shrug. "There are plenty more where they came from. And they should be happy to die for their king."

"Only if the King is worth dying for," Merlin snapped. Sometimes he really hated Vortigern. The man didn't seem to care about his people at all.

"Mind you, it has been difficult to find new soldiers," Vortigern said crossly. "And that's very annoying because I might need an even bigger army soon ..."

The King suddenly shut up. Merlin could tell that he was keeping something secret. The soldiers and the druids and the servants looked nervous. Some of them began to edge towards the door.

"Come on, out with it," Merlin said. "Tell me the whole story."

And this was what had happened. After the fight with Hengist and his men, Vortigern wanted to build a huge monument where the battle had been. It was a reward for the dead warriors, a way to show they'd never be forgotten. But Vortigern wanted the monument quickly. Instead of getting his men to build what he wanted, he sent them to Ireland to steal a monument that was there already – a great big stone circle on a mountain. The Irish tribes hadn't let them take their stones away.

"In fact, they were very nasty to us," said Vortigern. "Their leader – his name is Dagda, I think – sent me a horrid message. But I didn't take much notice."

"What did the message say?" Merlin murmured. A cold chill ran down the back of his neck.

"Oh, there was a lot of shouting about how I didn't have the right to invade Ireland," said Vortigern. "And how he was going to join forces with Hengist."

Merlin groaned softly. This was bad news. All at once Vortigern had doubled the number of Britain's deadly enemies. Dagda was a great chief like Hengist, and the Irish warriors were as wild and fierce as Hengist's Saxons.

"Did he say when the two armies were joining up?" asked Merlin. "And where?"

"Yes, he did," Vortigern said. He was happy now – and trying to be helpful. "Midsummer Day is when they plan to meet, on the great plain by the river, just where I wanted to build my monument. But we don't need to worry about that ... do we?"

"You don't, but I have to," Merlin muttered, and swept out of the room.

It was even more important now for Merlin to find that ring of power. And he didn't have much time. Midsummer Day was very soon ...

There was someone who could help him. Merlin left the castle and headed for the cave that lay under it. He ran down some stone stairs. There was a shining pool on the floor of the cave.

"Hello, Merlin," growled the great red dragon. "I've been expecting you."

Chapter 3
Dragon Flight

No matter how many times Merlin saw the red dragon, he was always amazed by how beautiful and how big it was. It was enormous – a massive beast with huge wings, sharp fangs, hooked claws and a long tail. The dragon rose from the pool and water dripped off its red skin. Its head moved close to Merlin.

"It's good to see you," the dragon growled softly. "But I can tell from your face that you don't feel it's good to be back. You've heard the news."

"I have, old friend," said Merlin, and gave the dragon's warm, smoky head a stroke. "I feel like giving up and going back to the farm ... What am I going to do now?"

"Didn't you find The Lady of the Lake on your journey?" said the dragon.

"I did. But it took a long time," said Merlin. "And all she told me was that I'd need a ring of power to make my magic stronger. She didn't tell me where I could get one. Do you know?"

"Alas, I have never heard of such a thing," the dragon murmured sadly.

"Oh, well, I'll just have to keep thinking," said Merlin. "Right now, I'd like to find out what Hengist and Dagda are up to. Do you fancy a little outing?"

"Why, of course, Merlin!" said the dragon, its eyes bright.

Moments later Merlin was sitting on the dragon's back, like a rider on a horse. He raised a hand, pointed at the roof of the cavern, and muttered a spell.

The roof cracked open, and soon there was a gap big enough for the dragon to pass through. The great beast flapped its wings and flew out of the cave.

Merlin looked down at the court-yard far below. Lots of tiny people were running around and screaming. Merlin didn't have time to worry about them. He had far more serious things on his mind.

"Let's check on Hengist first," he shouted into the dragon's enormous ear.

The dragon nodded, and turned to the east. Soon they were flying over the lands

the Saxons had taken from the Britons. Merlin gave a sigh. There were rich farms with big fields of crops, villages full of homes – and he could see even more Saxon ships arriving on the eastern coast.

"That must be Hengist's army," said Merlin as he saw a dark mass of men. They were marching together into a great hill fort. The dragon flew low so Merlin could get a closer look. Merlin saw a tall warrior. That had to be Hengist. The Saxon chief shook his sword at the dragon, and his army roared a battle cry.

The sun glittered on their weapons and armour, and soon arrows were whizzing upwards. Merlin knew he and the dragon were safe – they were flying too high to be hit. But he was still filled with gloom. Hengist's army was enormous and the men looked tough and hard.

"Come on, I've seen enough," said Merlin. "Let's go and check on Dagda."

The dragon turned steeply and flew off into the west. The land whipped past below them, then the sea, and at last they were over the green fields of Ireland. What Merlin saw there made him feel even more gloomy. Dagda had called together an enormous army, and Merlin saw a great fleet of long-ships waiting on the coast to take it to Britain.

Dagda and his men saw Merlin and the dragon high above, and shot arrows at them just as the Saxons had. But the Irish arrows came no closer than those of the Saxons. The dragon flew on, while Merlin scanned the world below. He saw something odd on a mountain below him. There were some big stones standing in a pattern near the top of the mountain.

"Take me down there!" Merlin shouted, and the dragon did as he was told.

Moments later they landed on the steep side of the mountain. Merlin jumped off the dragon and walked up to the huge stones. There were lots of them. Each one was twice as tall as a man, and they had all been cut into the same shape. The most interesting thing was that they were all arranged in a ring round the very top of the mountain.

"I'm sure this is the stone circle Vortigern tried to steal," said the dragon. "How did he ever think he'd get it back to Britain? It would be impossible."

Merlin didn't answer. He could feel his skin tingling, as it always did when he used his magical powers. Blue sparks leapt from his finger-tips as he walked into the centre of the circle. He held a hand up ... and a bolt of energy jumped from him, then passed from stone to stone until all the stones were joined by a soft, humming ring of blue light. Merlin put his hand down by his side and smiled.

"I think I know now what a ring of power is!" he said as he ran out of the circle and up to the dragon. "These stones are as old as the hills and full of magic, and they make my magic stronger ..." Then he stopped and looked down at his hands. The blue sparks were gone, and the tingling in his skin had vanished.

"What's wrong, Merlin?" asked the dragon. "You look upset."

"I think the magic only works when I'm inside the circle," groaned Merlin. "That's no good – I can't take the magic away when we leave, can I?"

"No, Merlin," said the dragon, "I don't think even your powers can bring the magic

away with you. But perhaps there are other stone circles, other rings of power that you could go to."

Merlin thought for a moment. "The problem is that I need to have a ring of power in one special place – the place where Hengist and Dagda are going to meet. That's where I must fight them and win."

"I see what you mean," said the dragon. "Then you'll just have to build your own stone circle."

"You're right," said Merlin. "But first I must find the right stones for it."

Merlin smiled. He knew just the right person to ask.

Chapter 4
The Keeper of the Books

They flew back to Vortigern's castle, and Merlin went to see the chief druid. The druid looked like something from a nightmare – a horrible old man with mad eyes, dirty white hair and a long white beard. When Merlin first met him, he'd been scared of him. But he soon found out the druid wasn't scary at all. He just looked bad.

"Don't blame me for what happened!" the old man cried as soon as he saw Merlin. The great red dragon standing behind the young wizard scared the chief druid even more. "I told the King not to attack Hengist," the old man added. "I knew you'd be so cross with him ..."

"Don't worry about it," said Merlin. "I'm sure you did your best," but he didn't believe anything the chief druid ever said. "I've come to have a look in your magic books."

The chief druid had another job. He was the Keeper of the Books in Vortigern's castle. It was his job to take care of all the old books and scrolls in the King's library. It had been in one of those books that Merlin had read about The Lady of the Lake. Was there another book or scroll that could help him find the magic blue stones he needed?

The old man looked hard at Merlin. "Er ... what are you looking for?" he asked.

"I'm trying to find some special stones. I think they're called blue stones," said Merlin. That's what The Lady of the Lake had told him, after all.

"You've come to the right place," said the chief druid. He grinned and Merlin saw all his bad teeth. "I've got the perfect book for you ..."

He scuttled off into the library, and Merlin followed him. The red dragon was too big to get through the door so he curled up outside to wait. It was dark and gloomy inside the library. The shelves were packed with books and scrolls. The chief druid began to pull books down and open them, making enormous clouds of dust.

"Ah, here it is!" said the chief druid at last. He held up a very old book with rubbed and faded old gold letters on the leather cover. 'A History of the Stones of Britain.'

"I'm afraid it's all written in Latin. Would you like me to translate it for you?"

"I think I'll be OK," said Merlin as he took the book from the chief druid.

Merlin had always been good at learning languages. He could speak his own British language, of course, but he also knew Latin and Saxon, and Irish. He went to sit in a dark corner of the library with the book, and soon found an entry about blue stones – and where to find them.

"Magic stones ..." he murmured to himself, "best for building rings of power ... the far west of Britain... in the mountains called Preseli." Merlin slammed the book shut and chucked it to the chief druid, who just about caught it. "Thanks," Merlin grunted, and strode out.

"You're very welcome, Merlin," said the chief druid, keen to do anything to help. "Let me know if there's anything else I can do for you. I'm always happy to help ..."

But Merlin wasn't listening. He was already on the dragon's back and they were flying up into the air and heading west again. A little later, they landed in a strange, lonely spot in the Preseli Mountains. There was a giant crack in the side of a mountain, almost as if another powerful wizard from a different time had hit it with a bolt of lightning. Stones and slabs of rock had fallen off the mountain and lay in heaps in the valley.

"The blue stones are here. I can feel it," Merlin whispered. The tingling in his skin was stronger than ever, and blue sparks crackled from all his fingertips.

He jumped off the dragon and ran over to the nearest stone. It was enormous. When Merlin looked at it closely, he saw it did have a light blue tint. Merlin put his hands on the surface, and felt magic power flowing into him.

"That's good," said the dragon. "But you'll need to cut out lots of these stones, and then get them to the plain by the great river. How will you do it?"

Merlin stood back and thought. Then he lifted his hand up and pointed at a stone. Blue sparks jumped from his fingers. The stone rose slowly off the ground. Merlin moved it a little way ... then let it crash down. He couldn't move it any further – but he had shifted it a bit. That was all that mattered.

"I want you to go back and tell Vortigern to send as many of his men here as he can," said Merlin. "I can lift the stones so that the men can get log rollers under them. Then we'll push the stones down to the nearest

beach, load them on boats, sail them up the great river – and unload them on the plain."

"What a clever idea, Merlin!" said the dragon. "I'll do just as you say ..."

Merlin knew it was a clever idea, and he was sure it would work. He only hoped he'd have the time to finish the job. Even with the help of his new magic powers, they'd need many days of hard work to get the blue stones to the great plain by the river. And then he'd still have to build his ring of power – and Midsummer Day was getting closer all the time ...

For once, Vortigern didn't let Merlin down. He sent him plenty of men, and lots of boats, too. Merlin worked harder than he'd ever done in his life, cutting out the stones, raising them so the men could get them on the rollers and then checking they were

safely loaded on the boats. The days passed in a blur.

He had to do the same thing at the other end. The boats had to be unloaded, the stones put on more rollers and then moved on to the great plain. That took even longer, but at last all the stones were in place – a giant stack of huge blue stones waiting to be made into a ring of power.

But now it was the night before Midsummer Day, and the enemy had come, ready for battle ...

Chapter 5
Battle on the Plain

Merlin stood next to the stack of blue stones as the sun set. Hengist's army was camped on one side of the great plain, and Dagda's men were on the other. Vortigern's much smaller army was camped between them. Smoke rose from camp fires, and the warm summer air was full of the sound of the soldiers in all three armies talking as they got ready for the battle. Merlin could hear the chink of their weapons and their horses snorting and neighing.

"I wish you hadn't sent that dragon back to the castle," muttered Vortigern. He was standing behind Merlin. "We're going to need all the help we can get."

"He has a battle of his own to fight," Merlin said softly. He remembered the first time he'd met the dragon. Every day in his cave, the red dragon fought a great white dragon, who was the Saxons' creature. Did the red dragon have to fight a green dragon too now – from the Irish?

"Oh well, I suppose you know what you're doing," said Vortigern with a shrug. "Er ... you do know what you're doing, don't you? Have you got a plan?"

Merlin turned to look at the king of the Britons, and gave a sigh. "Yes, Vortigern, I do have a plan," he said. "And you'll get to know about it too, all in good time."

"Couldn't you give me some kind of clue?" said Vortigern. "Just a little one? I think your plan has something to do with these stones, but I don't see how you're ..."

"Leave me, Vortigern," Merlin snarled suddenly. All at once, he couldn't take any more of this silly king.

"Of course!" squeaked Vortigern, spooked by Merlin's flashing eyes. The King backed away so quickly he nearly tripped over, but Merlin took no notice of him.

The young wizard had far too much on his mind to worry about Vortigern. Merlin's plan was simple – it had to be. He had run out of time. He had to build his ring of power before the sun rose again in the morning. He didn't think Hengist and Dagda would attack before then. But he didn't know if he could get the ring of power built in just one night – it seemed impossible.

But then being a wizard seemed impossible only a little time ago. And he'd done many things since he'd been a wizard. Maybe he should just trust himself – or rather, trust the power he could feel growing inside him. The stack of blue stones he stood next to was humming and giving off a soft, but very definite blue glow ...

Merlin slowly lifted his hands up – and three of the blue stones seemed to jump up, almost as if they wanted to obey him. Merlin made them dance and weave around each other. Crackling blue energy flowed from his finger-tips like a waterfall. Then he planted two stones in the ground. They landed with a *thud!* and Merlin put a third stone across the top of them with a loud *crunch!*

Merlin smiled. What he needed to do might not be as hard as he'd thought ...

It still took him all night. He made the whole stack of blue stones dance. The great plain was full of blue lightning flashes but no one saw what Merlin was doing. It was only when the sky began to get lighter that the armies began to make out a weird new shape standing right in the middle of the plain.

There was a massive ring of stones now between the armies. The Irish and Saxon warriors looked at it. They scratched their heads and muttered to themselves. Hengist and Dagda rode across to talk to each other. They pointed at the ring. Vortigern was amazed by it too, and crept up to peer through one of the arches with the chief druid.

"What are you playing at, Merlin?" said Vortigern. "I know I wanted to build a monument here for the battle we lost, but now we've got another battle to fight and I need a bit of help with fighting it."

Merlin was standing on a big square slab of blue stone in the middle of the ring. He turned to face the east. The sky was getting brighter, and he knew the sun would soon rise over the plain. A light breeze swished over the grass of the plain and blew Merlin's long hair back from his face. His eyes shone.

"Just get the men in place," he said. "Our enemies are about to attack."

Vortigern looked round. Merlin was right. "Get ready, men!" he yelled, and the army of the Britons formed a circle round the ring. They pointed their spears outwards at the Saxon and Irish armies. They were only just in time – the Saxons and the Irish crashed into them. Soon the plain was full of the sounds of men fighting.

The Saxons were grim, tough warriors. Their eyes glittered with hate over the rims of their wooden shields as they jabbed with their spears or stabbed with their swords. The Irish warriors had tattoos all over their faces and their bodies. They fought like demons from another world. Blade clanged on blade, blood flowed, and the Britons were slowly pushed back ...

"We can't hold them back!" shouted Vortigern at last. "Do something, Merlin!"

But Merlin waited until the moment was right. As the sun rose into the sky, a ray of light shot down from it and hit the blue stone Merlin stood on. Blue energy crackled out of him and leapt onto the stones. The blue light sped round the stones in a circle, joining them together in a great humming ring of power. Then Merlin lifted his hands up – and flattened the Saxons and the Irish as if they were a field of corn blown down in a great storm.

Many warriors were killed at once. The rest picked themselves up and ran for their lives, screaming in panic. The Britons shouted with joy and chased after them.

"I don't know how you did it, Merlin, but I'm impressed!" said Vortigern. "That's the end of them! I'll bet they won't mess with us ever again."

Merlin didn't say a word. He was looking at Hengist. He stood at the rim of the great plain, and stared back at the ring of stones. The Saxon chief lifted his sword in anger at Merlin and Vortigern.

Then he turned and slowly walked away. Merlin knew that he might have won this battle, but the long war wasn't over yet ...

There would be many more battles to come, and much more difficult ones too.

And what became of the ring of power Merlin had built on the great plain? Well, it still stands to this day. But we call it ...

Stonehenge ...

Our books are tested
for children and young people by
children and young people.

Thanks to everyone who consulted on
a manuscript for their time and effort in
helping us to make our books better
for our readers.

Find out how it all began in ...

YOUNG MERLIN

by Tony Bradman

**In a time of myth and a land of magic,
one boy will shape the future...**

Merlin has always known he's different from the
other boys. But he has no idea just how different.
Inside Merlin, lies power. Magic.

And that makes him a threat to the King...

www.barringtonstoke.co.uk